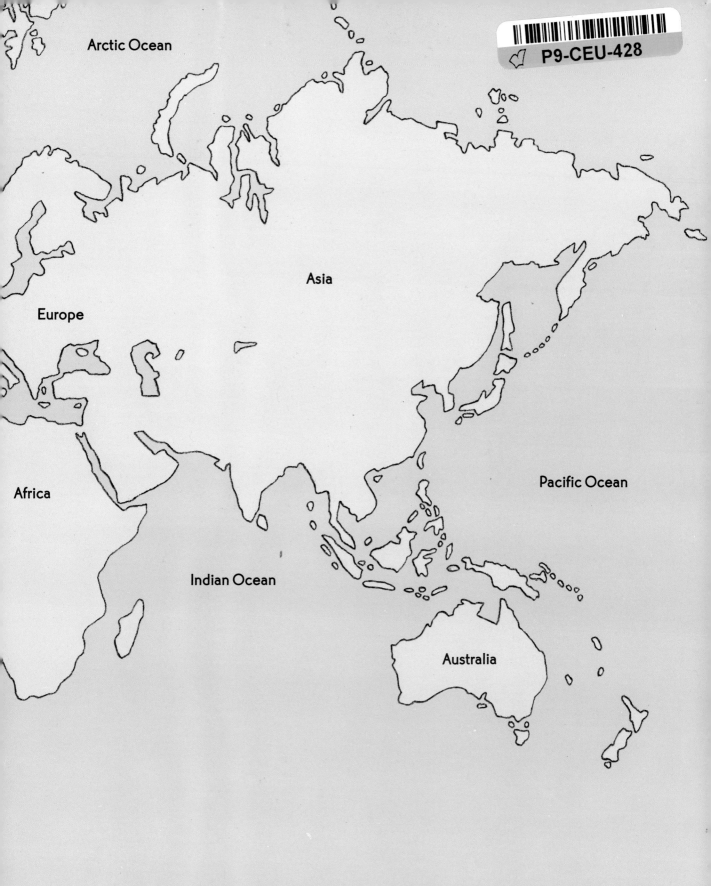

Arctic Ocean

Asia

Europe

Africa

Pacific Ocean

Indian Ocean

Australia

What Is Your Language?

What Is

Your Language?

Song by DEBRA LEVENTHAL

Pictures by MONICA WELLINGTON

Dutton Children's Books · New York

Song copyright © 1968 by Appleseed Music, Inc.   Notes and illustrations copyright © 1994 by Monica Wellington

All rights reserved.

Library of Congress Cataloging-in-Publication Data

Leventhal, Debra. What is your language?/song by Debra Leventhal;

pictures by Monica Wellington.—1st ed.   p.   cm.

ISBN 0-525-45133-1

1. Language and languages—Juvenile literature.   I. Wellington, Monica.   II. Title.

P124.L48 1994   93-10156   CIP   AC

Published by arrangement with Dutton Children's Books, a division of Penguin Books USA Inc.

375 Hudson Street, New York, New York 10014

Designed by Amy Berniker

Printed in USA

The art was done with gouache, watercolor, and color pencil on paper.

For Lydia, my little world traveler
. . .
Grateful thanks to Barbara Baker and Inge King, and the many generous people at
the United Nations Photo Library, UNICEF Picture Library, and national tourist offices
and consulates who helped me while doing research for this book.
—MW

Where are you going?
Please tell me now.
I'm off to make new friends,
All around the world.

Let's go!

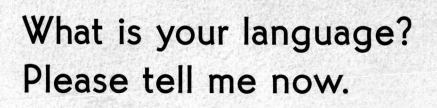

What is your language?
Please tell me now.

My language is English.
This is the way it sounds:

What is your language?
Please tell me now.

My language is German.
This is the way it sounds:

What is your language?
Please tell me now.

My language is French.
This is the way it sounds:

What is your language?
Please tell me now.

My language is Russian.
This is the way it sounds:

da

da

da

da

da

What is your language?
Please tell me now.

My language is Inuktitut.
This is the way it sounds:

ima

ima

ima

ima

ima

ima

What is your language?
Please tell me now.

My language is Japanese.
This is the way it sounds:

What is your language?
Please tell me now.

My language is Chinese.
This is the way it sounds:

shi

shi

shi

shi

shi

shi

shi

What is your language?
Please tell me now.

My language is Arabic.
This is the way it sounds:

na'aam

na'aam

na'aam

na'aam

na'aam

na'aam

What is your language?
Please tell me now.

My language is Swahili.
This is the way it sounds:

What is your language?
Please tell me now.

My language is Spanish.
This is the way it sounds:

Where are you going?
Please tell me now.
I've been on a long trip,
And now I must go home.

no

no

non

non

non

Don't go!

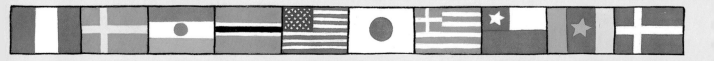

WHAT IS YOUR LANGUAGE?

Moderately

Words and music by Debra Leventhal

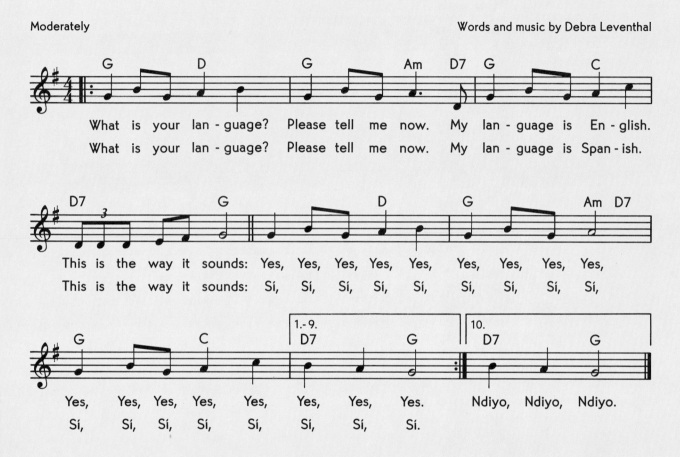

What is your lan - guage? Please tell me now. My lan - guage is En - glish.
What is your lan - guage? Please tell me now. My lan - guage is Span - ish.

This is the way it sounds: Yes, Yes, Yes, Yes, Yes, Yes, Yes, Yes, Yes,
This is the way it sounds: Sí, Sí, Sí, Sí, Sí, Sí, Sí, Sí, Sí,

Yes, Yes, Yes, Yes, Yes, Yes, Yes, Yes. Ndiyo, Ndiyo, Ndiyo.
Sí, Sí, Sí, Sí, Sí, Sí, Sí, Sí.

For the following verses, replace the name of the language

and the way to say *yes* with the words below:

Language	*This is the way it sounds*	*Language*	*This is the way it sounds*
German:	Ja, Ja, Ja	Japanese:	Hai, Hai, Hai
French:	Oui, Oui, Oui	Chinese:	Shi, Shi, Shi
Russian:	Da, Da, Da	Arabic:	Na'aam, Na'aam, Na'aam
Inuktitut:	Ima, Ima, Ima	Swahili:	Ndiyo, Ndiyo, Ndiyo

A NOTE ABOUT LANGUAGES

There are about five thousand different languages spoken in the world. Many languages are spoken only by relatively small numbers of people in specific geographic areas, while major languages are spoken by large numbers of people in wide-spread areas.

· · ·

ENGLISH is spoken throughout the United States, Canada, Great Britain, Ireland, Australia, and New Zealand. It is also used as a second language in almost every part of the world.

GERMAN is the official language of Germany and Austria, as well as one of the official languages of Switzerland. The German and English languages have many close connections.

FRENCH is the official language of France, and it is spoken in Belgium, Switzerland, Canada, the Middle East, Africa, and the Caribbean. French is a Romance language — a language that developed from Latin — as are Spanish, Portuguese, Italian, and Rumanian.

RUSSIAN is spoken in Russia and in many of the republics that were part of the former Soviet Union. It is the most important language of the large Slavic group of languages, which also includes Polish, Czech, Slovak, Ukrainian, and Bulgarian. Russian is written in the Cyrillic alphabet, which is based on the Greek alphabet.

INUKTITUT is spoken by the Inuit peoples, although the dialect varies from one area to another. Missionaries developed an Inuktitut syllabic writing system so that the Inuit could read and write their own language.

JAPANESE is the official language of Japan. The Japanese language is not related to Chinese, but the Japanese did adopt the Chinese system of writing. The Chinese characters were later supplemented with two sets of phonetic, syllabic characters.

CHINESE has many dialects, but Mandarin Chinese is spoken by the majority of people in China. The dialects differ greatly in pronunciation, but the written language is the same. The writing system uses pictorial symbols, rather than symbols representing sounds, to represent objects, words, and ideas.

ARABIC is spoken throughout the Middle East and northern Africa. Modern spoken Arabic varies greatly from country to country, but the written language is standardized and extends beyond the main areas of the spoken language, to wherever the Islamic religion is practiced.

SWAHILI is an official language of Kenya and Tanzania, and it is spoken as a first language along the east coast of Africa and as a second language by millions of people across sub-Saharan Africa. There are many different varieties of Swahili in Africa.

SPANISH is spoken in Spain, as well as in almost all the countries of Latin America. Many people in the United States also speak Spanish. It is the most widely used Romance language in the world.

People have long been interested in having one language that could be spoken throughout the world and serve as a bridge between language groups for international communication. The most successful universal language is Esperanto, introduced in 1887 by Dr. L. L. Zamenhof, where yes is *jes* and no is *ne*.

The languages used in this book are all widely spoken, but if you want to research how to say *yes* and *no* in another language, you might look in your local library for bilingual dictionaries of many different languages.

A pronunciation guide for the foreign words in this book is included below, in parentheses.
The words in Russian, Inuktitut, Japanese, Chinese, and Arabic also appear in their own alphabets.

	Yes			No		
English	Yes			No		
German	Ja	(yah)		Nein	(nine)	
French	Oui	(wee)		Non	(no[n])	
Russian	Da	(dah)	Да	Nyet	(nee-yet)	Нет
Inuktitut	Ima	(ee-mah)	ᐃᒪ	Aaka	(ah-kah)	ᐊᑲ
Japanese	Hai	(hi)	はい	Iie	(ee-ay)	いいえ
Chinese	Shi	(shih)	是	Bu	(boo)	不
Arabic	Na'aam	(nam)	نعم	La	(lah)	لا
Swahili	Ndiyo	(ndee-yoh)		Hapana	(hah-pah-nah)	
Spanish	Sí	(see)		No		

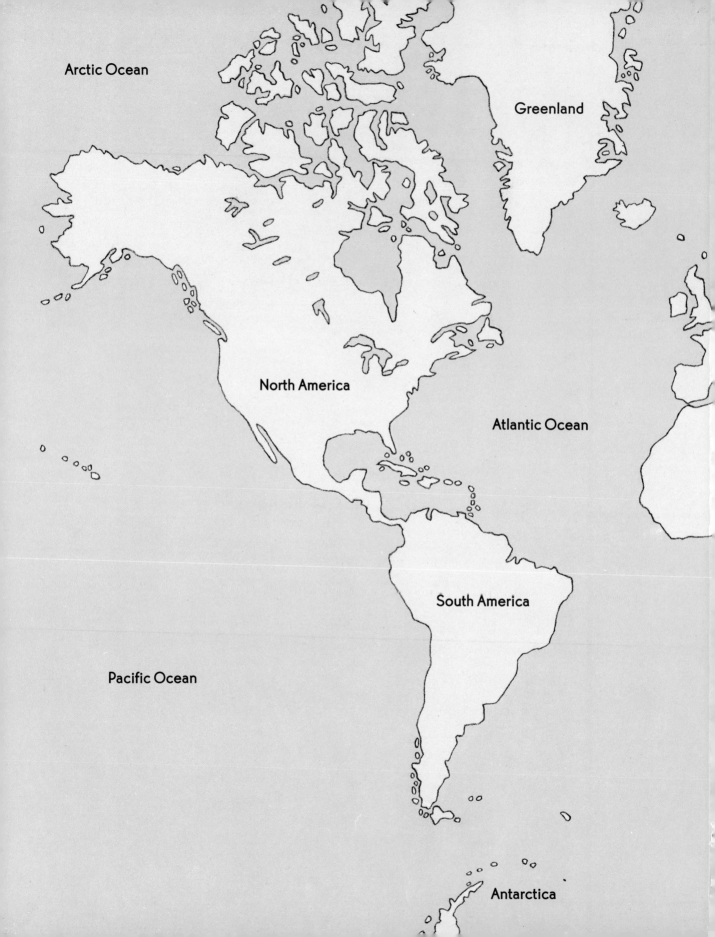